MW01223540

101 REASONS WHY IT'S GREAT TO BE SINGLE

KARLEEN DEE

authorHOUSE®

AuthorHouse™
1663 Liberty Drive
Bloomington, IN 47403
www.authorhouse.com
Phone: 1 (800) 839-8640

Published by AuthorHouse   01/13/2015

ISBN: 978-1-4969-6431-1 (sc)
ISBN: 978-1-4969-6430-4 (e)

ociety has somehow created the perception that singleness is bad; that being a single female means there is something wrong with you. Family and friends always have someone in mind that "you would love", or have suggestions on where you should be going to meet a new guy, and every second commercial is a dating site insisting they have the right formula to meet the man of your dreams. Even magazine articles written for the single woman target this relationship status in the most patronizing way possible. "Oh, you're single. Well we must then assume that you are also sad and lonely. Have no fear, here are 5 tips to make you feel better!"

Well, I'm here to tell you (or perhaps simply remind you), that the negative connotation of singleness is BS. We learn faster, discover ourselves more deeply and are overall happier and more content with life when we are single than when we are in a relationship with another human being.

You're probably reading this because your relationship has recently ended (or is looking to be over soon), or maybe you've never had a significant other and you're feeling a little bummed. Personally, I've had four long term relationships and none of them turned out to be right for me. However, these dating experiences have given me a whole new outlook on the single life and I've discovered various reasons why, contrary to popular belief, it is truly great to be single. In fact, I've discovered 101 of them, and I would like to share them with you. Why? Because you, are an amazing individual.

Before we get started on this wonderful journey together I would like to point out that I am not anti-relationship and these are not reasons why being in a relationship sucks. While some of these points may naturally come off as single vs. relationship simply due to the nature of this list, I am not about promoting negativity in any way. So, if you want to hate on your ex that's perfectly fine, vent all you want. Scream in your pillow, punch the wall, jump into a pool and thrash around in frustration, but you won't find any content here which cosigns your BS and helps you point a finger. I have no judgment on how you deal with your stuff, whatever works for you, I say "give 'er hell!" This list, however, is all positive. Let's forget about talking negatively about relationships and instead focus on the positives of singleness.

1.   WILDERNESS ADVENTURE
      You don't have to shave....anything! Grow out that pit stubble, let your legs sprout like prickly cacti, or embrace a full muff. Awkward, yes, but you don't care because you're single and you do what you want. Okay so that may be excessive, but you get the point – if the stubble grows out for a couple days, no one's complaining.

2.   EXTRA GARLIC!
      Love garlic? Onions? I sure do. If I'm in a relationship though I have to take into account that the other

person may not be too keen on dragon breath. So, I don't eat these things because I know that the smell and taste will linger in a very unpleasant manner.

When you're single you can eat all the onions and garlic you want and never have to worry about your stanky breath – unless you want friends... then you may want to be cautious of social situations as well.

3.   YOU KNOW WHERE IT'S AT
You have drawers but all your clothes are just shoved on top of each other into the shelves. In your bathroom, there are piles of makeup under your sink. It may look like you're a slob, but everything has its place and you know where to find it.

My boyfriend would always try to be helpful by tidying up the apartment. Which was great, but where the heck was my favorite shirt? It certainly wasn't on the pile on the floor where I left it!

When you're single you aren't wasting your time searching the house for your things – they are right where you left them.

4.   EXCESSIVE INDULGENCE
There is no sneaking in the door with your tub of quality cookie dough ice cream and feeling the cringe of resentment when your significant other asks to share. The tub is just too small for two spoons! When you're single you can inhale that whole thing, then sit

on the couch and feel fat with no one to judge you. Unzip those jeans and dig in sister!

5.   MORE SPACE FOR YOUR STUFF
If you're dating someone but you don't live together, chances are you're either lugging your belongings back and forth in a gym bag, or they've given you the coveted *drawer*. What the hell am I supposed to put in a drawer? I would look at my dinky little drawer stuffed with wrinkled garments, and look up at his huge, vast closet packed with 40 pairs of the same dress shirt in different colors. Then I would get all resentful – "why do you need that many dress shirts?!" Being single means my clothes are all in one place, and much less wrinkled.

6.   YOUR VERY OWN BED SPACE
The bed is all yours, do with it what you will. Sprawl out, starfish, or just thrash about randomly because you can (which does actually feel amazing. Seriously, go do it now).

What else? Oh yes, no worries about being throat punched in the midst of your enjoyment of ample dream space. True story – a boyfriend actually punched me in the night while he was sleeping. Apparently he was in a big wrestling match and forgot to inform me that I was fighting against him. According to him though, he won the fight and felt amazing. You better fucking have.

7.   LAUNDRY PROCRASTINATION
Sometimes when I do my laundry I dump it on the bed in preparation for putting it away. Sometimes I leave it there for a bit and tell myself that it needs to air out. Sometimes, since there is no one sleeping next to me, I just leave it there overnight. After all, I had a busy day and I just don't have the energy.

So, when I say sometimes, I mean all the time. When you don't have a person taking up the other side of the bed at night, there's really no rush on getting that laundry in the closet. I'm going to leave that laundry on the bed for a couple days until I'm damn well good and ready to put it away! I've actually gone an entire week just re-wearing the clothes from my clean laundry pile.

I should note that when you have guests over it's a good idea to get off your butt and put the laundry away. Or, just close the door. I'm pretty sure that's what they're there for anyway.

8.   BONUS INVITES
If anyone ever has one extra ticket anywhere they always invite you. You are the token single person there to save the day! Husband out of town and your friend won tickets to a local play? Sister's boyfriend broke it off before she could tell him about the hockey tickets she bought him? You are happy to take that seat! Heck... you may even buy the beer. Just kidding,

get the guy in line to buy it for you. After all, you are a sexy single minx.

9.   GUILT-FREE ADVENTURES
You do what you want when you want to. Need I say more!? (*insert finger snap from side to side*). Okay, okay so I will elaborate. I would always get invited out with my girls to do fun things, but I would feel bad about leaving my boyfriend at home. It wasn't his fault he didn't have female genitalia after all... so sometimes I would stay home with him and we would do our own thing, and other times I would go out but always feel that twang of guilt.

There is an air of liberation and freedom in accepting an invitation with no one to answer to. You go to that margarita night, painting party, or any of those other gender-specific-for-no-good-reason hang out nights and feel no guilt at all.

10.   NO RESTAURANT FOOD RESTRICTIONS
Dating a vegan? A lactose or gluten intolerant? That is awful. You're just fine with digging into a thick steak, a great chocolate milkshake or a loaf of banana bread – BUT, you don't eat these things because your significant other doesn't. How insensitive would you be eating a pizza in front of your love when even a small bite would bloat up their intestines like a balloon animal on Cindy's birthday? Well, if you're single you can eat whatever you want. Unless of course you're the one with the allergy, in which case, sucks to be you.

11. THE GOODS ARE YOURS

After splitting with a guy I lived with for over a year, deciding who owned what turned out to actually be quite difficult. Everything just blended together, especially those things I didn't see as too important. "Whose lamp is that?" "Who bought this side table?" "Was this from the last place you lived?"

When we broke up all of a sudden these became questions that needed to be answered. Not what I wanted to be dealing with at a time like that.

When you're single you don't have this problem – it's all yours!

12. A SILENT NIGHT

I had a boyfriend that would snore loudly. I mean really loudly. I could actually sleep in the next room and still hear him. So I tried lots of different things like wearing earplugs, taking sleeping pills, or rolling him on his side (or off the bed depending on how frustrated I was – "oops, sorry hun!").

Even when I did all that I would wake up in the middle of the night, unable to fall back asleep.

Do you know what lack of sleep does to you? Well, it makes you cranky. Certainly made me cranky anyway. I am a very positive and optimistic person, but as soon as my sleep is disturbed before my alarm goes off I become the evil dragon lady.

Now that I'm single I have a wonderful, uninterrupted sleep – no earplugs, and no dragon lady.

13.   AVOIDING RANDOM ANGER

Have you ever had those times when your significant other is angry at something you've done and you have no idea why they are angry, but they won't tell you why because – guess what? "You should know". I used to think that only girls did this, but no sir, one of my boyfriends did this all the time. This would cause lots of fights because I am a straight-forward, to-the-point type of lady (Sagittarius for the astrology lovers out there), which means I would tell him that he was being ridiculous and that I wasn't playing his mind games. Which needless to say, only made him angrier. Now that I am single, the only things I should know are the things that I already know!

14.   YOU KNOW WHERE YOUR JUNK'S AT

So this point relates to junk in a sexual nature. I know I said this isn't a book about knocking relationships, and I promise I won't start ranting here. It's just fact - when you're single, you know where your junk is and who you're sharing it with. You don't need to worry about your significant other leaving the relationship to "pursue spiritual enlightenment" only to find out that's actually just the name of the stripper he's been seeing for the last few months.

15. OWN THE THRONE
When living with my ex I would often get up in the middle of the night to pee. I would either have to turn a light on to check, or feel around to see if the seat was down (which yes, was so gross). So of course, I started nagging. I knew I sounded really annoying but I couldn't stop, it really bothered me! So I would nag, and he wouldn't do anything different and that was that.

When you're single, you know it's always down. No surprise bum-dunking in the middle of the night.

16. GET DRUNK AND DIRTY
(Note: this is only for adults. If you are a youngin' please do not get drunk and/or dirty). For the rest of us - You can get drunk and sleep with someone and not feel guilty about it! Go ahead, get wasted, hook up with that bartender that's cute in the right light and sneak out in the morning before he wakes up. Sure, you may feel cheap and used for a brief moment, but we both know this will be one of those "remember when" stories you share with your girls. After all, you don't make memories sitting at home.

17. SAVE YOUR HOLIDAY SKRILLZ
No need to buy expensive gifts on holidays. Seriously, between Valentine's day, his birthday, Christmas, our anniversary, and those other random holidays I swear he invented like his pet geckos first hibernation cycle, how was I supposed to keep coming up with gift

ideas!? Until they choose to bundle all the holidays together in a one-time money saver package I am much more content being single, thank you!

18. LET IT HANG LOW
     Okay so I really just liked the visual on that title but truth is this goes gals just as much as guys – especially because I'm of the lady variety and I love my naked time. You're single, you live alone, so why not be naked in your own home? Don't pretend like you don't know what I'm talking about you dirty bird. Also, a sex therapist told me one time that not wearing underwear at night is best – so I'm really just following doctor's orders.

19. ONESIES
     Oh yes I said it! Those button-up pajamas that no one would ever consider sexual? You OWN that when you are single. While I am all for being naked and letting things hang loose, there is a thing called winter where this just isn't possible (unless you are super rich and can afford things like heat). In those times, just slip on your onesie and you will feel not only warm and cuddly, but also sexy in a liberated I-wear-what-I-want sort of way.

20. CATCH MORE ZZZ'S
     I have absolutely no problem heading to bed at 8pm on a weekday. In fact, I get an odd satisfaction from getting in more than 9 hours of sleep. Could I do that with a boyfriend in the house? No way. When you're

single you can sleep on your schedule, even if that schedule is ridiculous.

21.   GET 'ER DONE
You have greater life aspirations when you're single because you're focused on one person (you), rather than two. This one hits home for me because when I'm in a relationship I always try really hard to please the other person and forget about myself and my personal growth. I push myself to achieve a lot more when I'm single. I'm focused on what I'm doing in life and how I can achieve more.

This may be truer for some than others. For me, I thrive on independence. When a relationship ends, it's over. No going back. So immediately I move on and start looking at how I can be happier and more independent. This is usually in my state of shock – I have no idea what else to do other than keep moving.

For others, they can't thrive without someone by their side, in which case, you grab that best friend of yours that you pushed away after you started dating your significant other. You know they are always there for you, because that's what best friends are best at! Pull them close and thrive, you amazing individual.

22.   SOAK UP THE SUN
Vacation whenever you want wherever you want (yes, I mean Vegas!). Depending on your significant other you can usually get away with going on a trip with

your besties, but we both know that even if they say it's cool that you go away without them, and no matter how long you've been together, there's always that unspoken resentment simmering under the surface.

Trips with my gal pals have always been an amazing time. We were wild, liberated, and yes even stupidly intoxicated. Trips with boyfriends have also been fun, but just not the same.

I won't always have the ability to just run away with friends and be ridiculous. Someday I will probably end up getting married, possibly more than once. Those relationships are serious, and committed, and scary. So for now, I'll embrace it while I can!

23.   WILD AND FREE
Even the most self-assured of us experience that twang of jealousy when our significant other is talking to an attractive person, or maybe just talking about an attractive person ("yeah I know she has a nice butt, that is because she is a freaking movie star and you can't get her anyway so shut up"). We can't help it, it's in our DNA to want to protect what we care about and we make things up even when nothing is going on which make us seem crazy.

I'm a social butterfly, so I talk to guys all the time. None of it means anything, I just like talking to people. Yet, when I would see my boyfriend doing the same thing my mind would start racing and I would lose it.

Being single means avoiding that pit in your stomach that forms when your head starts saying "what if"...

24.   FOREIGN SHNIGGITS
What is a shniggit you say!? A shniggit is a small fleck of something, anything. Those moustache trimmings he leaves in the sink? Shniggits. Those clumps of shaving cream on the bathroom counter? Shniggits. Those pieces of nothing that the vaccum seems to leave behind on purpose to taunt you? Those are shniggits too!

When you're single the only shniggits you need to worry about are your own. Somehow they are much less gross when they are yours.

25.   EMBRACE THE FIRST DATE
The giddy first date feeling – need I say more?! You meet somewhere, chat a little bit (these days sometimes just online), and you decide to go on a date. You likely already have butterflies from your initial conversations, and you have high expectations for your first date encounter.

When you meet in person, if the date goes amazing those butterflies burst into overload and you are on cloud nine! If the date goes terribly, it's still a great story to tell your friends.

26.   A VISITOR IN YOU OWN CITY
The first date always carries pressure of doing something exciting. This can be nerve wracking for

some, but it helps you do things that you wouldn't normally do – a new coffee shop? Race car driving? Seasonal month events?

All of a sudden you are learning new things and discovering adventures in your own city that you never knew about before. Congratulations you single devil, you're now the friend that knows the best spots to hang out and the most exciting places to visit.

27.   OWN YOUR CORN
No sharing popcorn at the movie theatres - that shit is all yours. Extra butter? Of course. Cheese powder? Why not, load it on. Your friend wants some? Too bad, we're not dating - go buy your own you leech! - PS get me a magazine on the way back in...

My ex would always want to share popcorn. I guess he thought it was romantic or something, but it was really just more annoying than anything. He had giant man hands which took up the whole bag so I would have to ninja my way in there just to get some.

Now I get my own popcorn – heck sometimes I even stick both hands in just because I can. (*popcorn shower moment*).

28.   CLEAN AND LEAN
Sure, after a breakup you'll probably be chowing down on junk food for breakfast lunch and dinner...but after the pain subsides and you realize you can actually live just fine without someone at your side you'll regain

your ground and get back to your normal. One of your normals is not matching the eating habits of your significant other. Let's face it, couples bring each other down in terms of eating habits. We get comfortable, we indulge and we let ourselves go.

One of my boyfriends was big into the gym and always wanted to eat more to get bigger. That meant meat and carbs, and lots of it. Pizza, pasta, lasagna - It all looked so good! I couldn't help but indulge when it was sitting right in front of me, and needless to say, my waistline suffered.

Being single means not having cheesy goodness around all the time. Single and slim!

29.   LIGHTS, CAMERA, ACTION!
It's Friday and you feel like staying in and watching a movie to relax and unwind from a busy week. What movie do you want to watch? Ooh shit you're single, you can watch whatever movie you feel like. Action isn't your thing? Well you aren't fucking watching it then.

30.   YOUR TV YOUR WAY
Same goes with TV shows. In my experience, the TV shows that my significant other likes to watch and those that I like to watch are completely different.

I had one boyfriend who loved sports. Sports were always on. Growing up in a family of women, this was not high on my list of things I was into. So we would compromise – he could watch his sports if he watched my cooking show with me afterwards. Neither of us were completely satisfied with this situation.

Cooking shows are now on my TV pretty much all the time. I watch them when I am cooking and pretend that I am the Chef Master (because let's face it, no one makes mushroom soup quite like THIS gal). Seriously though, I have actually become better in the kitchen due to my increase in cooking show watching. Thank you, singleness.

31.   STAY IN BED

Indulge in guilty pleasures! This includes staying in bed for an entire day watching a whole season of your favorite TV sitcom while eating a box of chocolates. Does that seem excessive? Then you've been in a relationship too long and need to come back to reality where some days are meant to be wasted.

There was one Sunday recently where I had no plans, and didn't have anything I needed to do. So, I got up, I made breakfast, and then I went back to bed for a morning nap. I woke up later for lunch, then watched three Christmas movies in a row. By the time the day was over I had been horizontal for 95% of it and had accomplished nothing. Stress levels were an all-time low and I felt fantastic. I have never had a day like this in the past when I was dating someone – must be a single gal thing.

32.   MIX UP YOUR MEALS
Eat whatever you want for dinner – there are no rules when it comes to meals at your house. You aren't sharing and you don't need to explain why you're eating what you're eating. Feel like cereal at 6pm? You go right ahead you single saucy devil.

A lot of the time I don't have time to go grocery shopping, so I will just make something up. Recently I had a can of chunky beef soup over egg noodles. I didn't mind it and I didn't judge myself, but there is no way I could have gotten away with feeding that to someone else.

33.   NO RANDOM MESS
No cleaning someone else's mess. For some reason I don't mind my own mess – I consider that toothpaste on the counter as part of the bathroom aesthetic. Fung Shui, if you will. As soon as it is someone else's mess though, it gets annoying as hell.

My boyfriend would always leave his dirty dishes in the sink. He would come home from work, make food, leave the mess on the kitchen counter and the dirty dishes in the sink, and then plop down on the couch and zone out on the TV. Before I even came in the door I knew they would be sitting there, staring at me. Mocking me.

I have my own dirty dishes to deal with now, but for some reason I just don't give myself the same flack.

34.   WHAT DO YOU WANT?

Ever been asked what your preference is for a movie, or restaurant, or shopping mall, and actually had no idea what to say? If you've been in long term relationships like me, you're so used to taking into account what your partner wants that you haven't really thought about what would really make you happiest. Rather than focusing on someone else, when you are single you really get to grow as a person and discover your own likes and dislikes.

35.   ANTI IN-LAW

So, you need to deal with your nagging parents now that you don't live at home. "When are you coming for dinner?!" "Are you going to pay us back any time soon?" Nothing I can do about that, sorry. However, the headache doubles as soon as you are in a relationship.

My boyfriend's parents would always want us over for dinner, and so did mine. If we lived up to their ideals that would be two nights every week taken by parental dinner nights. That is a lot!

My parents understand when I tell them I'm just too tired. You can't do that with someone else's parents, they would just think you were an asshole.

When you're single there are only one set of parental obligations to shirk out of.

36.　TREAT YOURSELF

Feel like buying 10 pairs of shoes today? Go for it! If you have the money, that is – I am not advocating debt for shoes. In a relationship, your partner seems to feel like they have a right to comment on all of your purchases (even more so if you share a bank account). I'm not saying they don't have the right to – you probably don't need 17 pairs of the same shoe, I'm just saying that when you're single you don't need to explain why you're obviously right. Also, you have so much more closet space to fill now!

37.　FINDING YOUR ZEN

No matter how similar you are to someone you will always have your differences, and that means fighting. Fighting is exhausting – you both advocate that your view is right, and then feelings escalate and the energy turns tense and negative. Eventually you probably work through it but the whole process is excessive and tiring. Or maybe you won't work through it, in which case it's a damn good thing you're reading this list, hey?!

38.　MIX UP YOUR FLAVORS

Get a little bit of everything – date a really smart guy, then a dumb jock with a six pack, then a dude with a really sexy accent. Sure he may not be Mr. Right, but he sure is fun for a little while! After one of my relationships ended I was overcome with a feeling of liberation and a need to get out and explore what the world had to offer. So, I downloaded a dating app. It was like a vending machine of men! A free vending machine that is, it wasn't some weird hooking service... anyways. There were so many of them! All looking for dates! Unfortunately, it didn't turn out well in the end. All the guys I talked to seem to be of the douche bag variety and really only wanted to get laid. It was a great experience though, and not one I would have had if I were in a relationship.

39.   BROS BEFORE HOS

Okay so I'm of the lady variety and therefore I do not advocate calling women hos, but it rhymes, so get over it. Anyway - once you get into a relationship your friend circle dwindles. Your significant other becomes your best friend. That's cute, but it doesn't replace the amazing relationships you have with your ladies.

I always seem to push my friends away. I want to spend all my time with my boyfriend and eventually we get so close that I don't see any of my ladies anymore. The great thing about friends though, is that when my relationships end they are always still there. Love those bitches.

40.   SEXY MAGIC

Newly single? You just got hotter. Once you own your singleness, you carry an air of independence about you that is envious to those in relationships and extremely attractive to those that aren't. You are fucking independent – own it!

Have you ever seen someone who clearly just has it all together? That fit, attractive woman in the glasses wearing a business suit, carrying her $5 coffee and strutting to an obviously important meeting, for example? Yeah, damn right she's single. Or was single for a while until she got all her shit together and found the perfect man.

41. NO POOP SMELL
Women are efficient at taking a #2. We get in, do our thing and get out. Guys take an entire magazine in there! What the heck are you doing?! They do their thing and let it sit there for 20 minutes – of course the room is going to smell after that.

When you're single, you only have to smell your own poop! Let's face it – our own just never smells as bad.

42. NO SHARING CHCOLATE
You get to eat the whole Twix bar – none of this "there's two pieces and two of us" garbage. This one actually relates to any type of chocolate bar that is split into pieces. Twix, Kit Kat, King sized Mars Bars...

Clearly I came up with this one while I was PMSing and when chocolate is of the utmost importance. At that time of the month, you want all the chocolate. Unrealistic amounts of chocolate, and no one is getting in your way.

43. BECOME A SOCIAL BUTTERFLY

    Don't have a dog? Borrow one. Dog walking is a great way to meet people (yup even the opposite sex). Nothing needs to come of it, in fact when you're newly single you shouldn't even talk to people you're attracted to - it just feels great to get out and be social. If you've been in a relationship for a long time this is great practice for getting out of your shell and meeting people – they have a dog and you have a dog! Instant conversation starter. All of a sudden you are single, confident and social – look at you go!

44. FUN WITH FLIRTING

    In addition to simply talking with random people to build your confidence, is of course, flirting. Flirting with guys at the gym, at the coffee shop, or wherever really. You're a sexy minx and you should smile at randoms, it's fun. Don't find them attractive? Who cares, just give it a whirl. It'll make you better at it the next time you do see someone you think is drool-worthy and enhance your confidence.

45. LESS FAKING IT

    Remember those orgasms you used to fake? Yeah, we both know you've done it. The longer you've been together, the more fake orgasms. It's just the way it goes. Well, not anymore. You know how to push your own buttons and you damn well sure know when it's happened.

46.   YOUR PAD YOUR WAY

Your apartment is all yours! Decorate it however you want –a bachelorette pad with ridiculous amounts of fruity scented candles, perhaps?

I am a decorator, I love decorating for holidays. Christmas time meant stockings, garlands, tinsel, lights –you name it! For some reason my ex thought that this was crazy. He used the word "excessive" a lot.

Well, now my apartment is as excessive as I would like. It's green for St. Patrick's, there are eggs everywhere at Easter, and yes of course I have millions of chocolates and cards plastered around for Valentine 's Day! It may be crazy, but it's all mine.

47.   RULE THE ANIMAL KINGDOM

Your ex didn't like cats? Well now you can have 7. Always wanted a dog but they didn't? Go for it, get your very own Rover. Who knows, they may just make a better partner than your ex did.

Personally, being a newly single lady I wanted to get out and be social. I didn't have time to be at home a lot so I didn't want to get an animal that needed me to be there, like a kitten or a dog. However, I did think some sort of companionship would be nice, so I bought a fish! Just a little Siamese fighting fish who was very easy to take care of, but was nice to come home to (and sometimes have conversations with, don't judge me).

48.   LESS HEADACHES
For some reason I had a lot of headaches when I was with my ex. They were probably invented by my sub-conscious to get out of sex or cleaning the house, but when we split up they miraculously disappeared. What a relief!

49.   RIDING THE SAME RIDE
After a while no matter how sexy your mate is, sex gets into a routine. Same position, same segue into new position, same finish. Booooring. It gets to the point where you really just don't feel like having sex. You know what's going to happen, and you're really not stoked on the idea. Even the most sexual of beings get into this lull.

Now that you're single it's a whole new ball game! You can mix it up with some fresh meat, or skip the whole thing all together and chill out on the couch with a pizza instead. The most fun you can have with your pants on – or heck, take 'em off. Who cares? You're single. In fact, I'm surprised you had them on in the first place.

50.   ROOM TO BREATHE
There is something liberating about having your own space with no one to share it with. For some reason, the apartment I lived in with my ex seemed much smaller than the one I live in now, even though they are the same size. Twice the stuff and twice the mess. Also, he always seemed to be where I wanted to be – both

in the kitchen making lunch for tomorrow, both in the bathroom getting ready. I felt guilty at how frustrated I would get with this.

The apartment I live in now feels enormous! Even the couch seems bigger. I feel like sitting on this side of the couch today, and the other side tomorrow. Guess what? I'm going to sit wherever the hell I want, because the space is all mine.

51.　NO DEALING WITH BOYS NIGHT

After a while in a relationship you really just want to get away from the other person for a while. So I understood when he would inadvertently say "sorry, you possess the incorrect genitalia for this evening".

I never minded when my ex would go out for boy's night. It meant I could have a nice relaxing evening at home by myself, maybe run a bubble bath a read a magazine. What irked me was when boy's night was at our place and he failed to remember to tell me until that morning. "Oh by the way hun, the guys will be coming by for poker later, hope that's okay". Oh, yeah, no problem, my vagina and I will just be hiding in the bedroom.

52.　NUNYA BIZNAZZ

Text freely without worrying about your significant other reading your text messages over your shoulder. Heck, you don't even need a passcode on your phone because no one cares what's on there. Oh, except your dirty photos – you should probably hide that shit in a photo vault.

I never had a passcode on my phone. They are annoying and I didn't think anyone would go through my phone – who would do that!? Well, my boyfriend at the time got curious and decided to take it upon himself to do a little snooping. Me trash talking about our relationship was apparently not on the list of things he wanted to read. Too bad buddy, you did this to yourself.

Being single means avoiding arguing about situations like this where you are clearly in the right.

53.   WAKE UP WHEN YOU WANT
There is nothing more annoying than your significant other getting up for work half hour earlier than you, and you being awake in bed waiting for your alarm to go off.

I'm a light sleeper so once I am awake, I'm awake. My ex used to work earlier than I did so for about 6 months of living together I was awake half an hour earlier than I needed to be, every week day. I would just lie there with my eyes closed listening to him getting ready, simmering in frustration. Clearly not his fault, but something I no longer have to worry about.

54.   NO SHARING THE BATHROOM
If you both have to get ready for work at the same time in the morning one bathroom becomes an issue.

Someone has to get up earlier to accommodate and avoid those elbow stabbing fights over the bathroom sink. When you're single you use the bathroom whenever and for as long as you want. Hell, have a morning dance party. Why wouldn't you?

55. BELT IT OUT
Sometimes I like to sing. Loudly. No matter how comfortable I am with my significant other I'm never as free and liberated as I am when I am singing in my apartment alone. I will often be found belting out cheesy girl music simply because I can. Side note: I do think that my neighbors hate me.

56. GET THERE QUICKLY
Doing anything always takes so much longer with two people, especially getting ready to go out somewhere. If you're living together and you both need to use the same shower, and share the bathroom, getting ready to leave the house takes so much longer. I also seem to date men that take longer than I do to get ready. What are you doing in there?!

It's not just getting ready, either. Picking a restaurant, shopping at the mall, and even travelling is so much faster when you're solo. Get that shit done.

57. MAKE YOUR BUCKET LIST
Sure you can have a bucket list when you're in a relationship but is it as awesome as the bucket list you would create if you were single?! It's yours and yours

only – be adventurous! When you're with someone else there's always that hesitancy on being as daring as you would be single. Can't put skydiving on there because your beau is scared of heights. Can't travel the world because you've got a limited budget and he just won't stay in a hostel. Guess what? You're single! Skydive all over the world you daring beauty.

58.   HIT UP A MUSIC FESTIVAL
Okay, so unless you're early 20's you're probably skimming over this, but you shouldn't! Festivals can suck if you are older, yes. BUT they can also be amazing for meeting new people and creating random drinking games you never thought possible. If you aren't in your early 20's just make sure to get their early and grab a spot in the corner. Also, bring sleeping pills to make sure you're still able to catch some Z's while the party animals stay up all night.

59.   NO BABY PRESSURE
His parents will bring up babies and you'll be like "what.....the......" [insert uncomfortable silence here], and then all of a sudden have to pee really badly and excuse yourself.

Especially where you're at an age where it makes sense – you're both late twenties, you make good money, you own your own home. Why aren't you making your parents grandparents yet!? Well, it's because I'm not ready and this whole conversation is giving me anxiety and I need to leave now, thanks.

If you want babies, you'll have babies one day. For now, you are single and you don't need to sweat it.

60.   WEAR UGLY CLOTHES
Come home from work and pull on those hideous sweats that make your ass look like puffy cottage cheese. Who cares, no one's watching!

In relationships I was never really that concerned with what I was wearing around my boyfriend (although I guess I should have been, maybe I would have gotten laid more often), but those clothes are nothing compared to the random garbage I get away with when single. Hangover breakfast with my girls is often accompanied by my largest, comfiest sweater and probably a pair of slippers. There is no judgement.

61.   WEAR THE HAIR YOU WANT
I've always wanted to be blonde even though I'm naturally very dark brown. I just wanted to try it to see what I would look like. So, one day I tried on a blonde wig and turned to my boyfriend and said "well, what do you think?" The look on his face said "take it off immediately you look like a member from a certain young boy band from the 90's".... if you catch my drift.

So, fine, I'm not meant to be blonde – but I could change it if I wanted just to give it a try without having to consult anyone about it or being compared to a prepubescent male.

62. AVOID THE PDA

Some people don't care about PDA. I am definitely not one of those people, but I have had boyfriends who certainly were. They always seem to do it in the most awkward areas too – for instance, in the middle of the mall hallway. There are people trying to walk past us and you're canoodling with me! Can't you see we are being rude!

Okay, so maybe I am being too anal. Either way, when you're single there are no awkward moments where you're stuck between not wanting to French your man in public, and also not wanting to offend them.

63. DUCK FACE AWAY

That duck face that no one likes you to make in photos? You're single, do whatever you want. We all know duck face is hilarious AND it starts a conversation. "Heyyyy saw that duck face guuurrrrlll, what's that all about? Where you be quackin??" I mean, types of guys like this probably aren't the best catch, but hey, I'm not one to judge on what you're into.

64. HAVE YOUR CELEBRITY CRUSH

We all have these anyway – but men seem to get jealous, even though it is a completely irrational jealousy.

I would pine over my celebrity crush whenever he would come on TV, and my boyfriend would get so jealous! It's not as if he can hear me yearning through the TV and ask me on a date (I mean, if he did I would've dumped my beau in a second but he doesn't need to know that).

When we're single we can crush, rave and post photos of any celebrity we want! They will be ours someday, we just need to casually visit where they live....

65.   YOUR MUSIC YOUR WAY
When you're single you can have the most ridiculous playlist imaginable and it's okay because you like all of that ridiculous music! No one to change the song you love or critique you on your song choice. Belt out that crazy tune.

For me, I have a playlist on my iPod that's called Guilty Pleasures, and it contains stupid girl songs that I absolutely love! They get me pumped and excited and overall just put me in a good mood. Boyfriend wants to listen to some tunes though? Well now I need to make a whole other playlist.

66.   LESSEN YOUR PREGNANCY SCARES
When you're single, you're probably using condoms. Unless you're a whore, in which case have fun with that herpes.... (Just kidding, no judgment here).

When you get into a relationship the trust builds and the STD worries fade, along with the condom usage. Hooray, no STDs but now your chances of getting pregnant have increased. If you're single, and use protection, there aren't any of those *oh shit* moments.

67. **HAVE A STAYCATION**
Invite the girls over and have a slumber party weekend in your pad, with tents and sleeping bags and cheesy girl movies without your significant other poking their nose in, asking "watcha doing now?"

I love having wine nights with my girls. Wine and baking cookies, wine and watching movies, wine and board games, or heck, sometimes just lots and lots of wine! Boyfriends are the worst at wine nights... they always fuck it up with beer. That's not the same!!

Being single I have lots of wine nights, and they are super delightful.

68. **OWN THE TITLE**
Just think about the title of *Miss* vs. *Mrs.* The connotation of *Miss* carries with it a sweetness that you just don't get with *Mrs.* When you're a *Mrs.* all of a sudden you're a hard-to-please woman of the household. *Miss's* on the other hand are just free-spirited innocent ladies of the land.

69. **RSVP ASAP**
No need to check with your significant other when you are invited out to things. If you want to go to an event, you go to the event. If it's not your deal then don't go.

I would always have to check with my ex when we were invited to things, and he would never get back to me. His hesitancy on making decisions was astounding.

Now, I can RSVP right away! If I want to go I say yes, and if it's not my thing I just make up some excuse. Simple as pie.

70.   BE SELFISH, HAVE FUN
Most likely, there will be a big part of your life where you do have a significant other. So, enjoy your time alone now, take advantage of all the fun single things you can do, and stop looking over the other side of the fence. There are a ton of great things about being single that you miss once you're in a relationship. Water your own lawn and you'll notice the grass is pretty luscious right where you stand.

71.   REDUCTION OF HORMONES
No excess testosterone from your man after he's pumped up from the gym and just has way too much energy for one human being. No putting up with irrational anger when they've run out of his favorite type of the sub. "WHAT?! NO MEATBALL!?" Yes, that happened.

The only hormones you need to deal with when you are single are your own (and let's face it, between the tears and the excessive chocolate indulgence we have enough to worry about).

72.   PUMP UP YOUR JAM
When you're single you have more time for yourself. You don't need to rush home to make dinner or worry about making plans with your significant other that

night – this frees up time for more things, such as exercise. I can go to work, hit the gym and be home to make dinner by 6pm. On weekends, I get up when I feel like it, hit the gym and then start my day. It's hard enough finding time for exercise with my own schedule, let alone having to work around someone else's too.

73.   SCHEDULE YOUR LIFE FOR YOU
My work gives us the option of working 9am-5pm or 7am-3pm. My 7am starts were killing me when my boyfriend wanted to stay up late watching movies because he didn't have work the next day. If I switched to 9-5 though, the day seemed much shorter. No boyfriend means I choose my schedule based on my needs, not his.

74.   WORK AWAY
Love your job? Looking to climb the corporate ladder? When you're single you're more likely to throw yourself into your work and advance in what you do, without having to deal with nagging from your significant other. Especially if you are in the cloud 9 stage of a relationship, where all you want to do is spend time with that person, you aren't going to waste extra hours of your day at the office. That means less hard work being put in and the less likelihood that you'll get a big raise during your next review. Congratulations hard working single fox, you're chances of riches have increased!

75.   SELF LEARNING

When you don't have someone else to do things for you, you've got to do it. Turns out girls can actually start their own BBQ and guys can do the dishes themselves – who knew!? A friend of mine recently became single and she renovated a whole room in the house by herself. I didn't know she had it in her, and honestly I don't think she did either! As soon as there isn't someone there to easily pass the buck off to for those things, you pick them up and realize you're more talented than you even knew.

76.   BEING REAL

No relationship is perfect, and there will be times when you fight with your other. Do you want to air all of your dirty laundry to your friends? Hell no, you don't want them to think your relationship is in trouble and you don't want them to look at your significant other negatively. So you put on a smile, say that things are great and you eventually get through it. When you're single there isn't any of that fakeness. Your problems can be shouted from the rooftops without the worry of making anyone else look bad – well, maybe just yourself, but your friends understand.

77.   YOU HOLD THE PURSE STRINGS

It's your own money, you know what is in your bank account and there is no one else making spending decisions that could affect both of you. He really needed a new set of tires for the truck? The online supplements were on sale so he needed to buy 10?

Well now you need to eat canned soup for the rest of the month in order to pay the rent.

Money management is much easier when there is only one person spending it.

78.   YOUR OWN GROCERIES

If you're lactose intolerant you don't want a tub of mint chocolate chip ice cream sitting in your freezer. If you've got a gluten allergy you don't need pasta, bread and cereal all over your kitchen. Your boyfriend can eat those things though, so he buys them and they just sit there, taunting you. You either stew in frustration or you end up giving in. In which case, not only do you pay the price, so does he.

When you're single, you only have groceries in your house that you are able to eat.

79.   SIBLING RIVALRY

It isn't just the in-laws that you need to worry about when you're in a relationship. Sometimes your significant other will have unnecessarily clingy brothers or sisters that just seem to be around all the time, and may even have a say in certain things within your relationship. All of a sudden the two of them are ganging up on you and you're questioning whether you've entered into a relationship with one person, or a brother-sister team. Scary.

Being single you only have your own siblings to worry about, no matter how annoying they may be.

80.   LEAVE ME ALONE

Sometimes I don't want to do anything. I come home from work and I just want silence. I want to walk in the door, put down my things, and just have a sit and think about what I should eat. When you're single you don't have to worry about answering the incessant texts from your other, or god forbid having a conversation about how your day was.

81.   FRIEND WHO YOU WANT

If you've got a boyfriend chances are he's not keen on having you hang out with other dudes. So you avoid them to keep him happy. Let's face it though, friends of the opposite sex are awesome. They have a unique perspective on things and you can flirt just a little bit without it going over the line and becoming weird.

I've always gotten along well with guys. I'm easy going and female drama just isn't really something I'm into, so I tend to sway towards the male variety. Boyfriends really hate that, and as soon as there is a boyfriend in the picture the guy friends dwindle. Unlike female friends, my guy friends and I are never really as close after the relationship ends either. I guess my hos be loyal after all.

82.   YOU'RE JUST FRIENDS?

Same goes the other way around, when you're the jealous one. There is a small raging fire on the inside as soon as your man tells you that he's going for coffee with his platonic friend Jenny that he went to University with, you know, "just to catch up". What....the...fuck.

When you're single you avoid all that jealous drama and fighting over his stupid lady friends that have no place talking to your man.

83.   YOU COMPRHEND TRUST

You can trust your family and you can trust your friends (unless you have shitty ones. In that case, probably get rid of them too). When you're single the people you keep close to you are usually very valuable. They are your rock.

When I'm hurting or going through something hard, I know that my family is always there for me. There is no judgment, I know that they won't go off and talk about it to anyone, and they always know exactly what I need. With boyfriends, I have always had a hesitancy to be completely open and honest without worry of judgment. With family I always know that's there.

84.   TIME FOR TV

Let's face it, there just isn't enough time in the day to catch up on your 5 favorite TV shows AND be dating someone. Satisfying the addiction of watching the last three episodes of your favorite show is too intense to pass up!

While living with a boyfriend I would come home from work, talk about my day, make dinner, and then sit down and watch a show. Now that I'm single I come in the door, take off my pants, grab some lucky charms and I'm on the couch. Save myself at least an hour which is then put towards another episode of TV goodness.

85.   AVOIDING OBLIGATIONS
There are certain things we do in a relationship that we do because we feel we have to. Cooking, cleaning, or taking out the garbage for example. If you don't do it, you know that your significant other is going to comment on it, especially if you got home first and therefore have more time to do these things.

When I'm single, sure I still have to do these things, but because there is no one telling me I have to or nagging me about it, it doesn't seem as big a deal.

86.   FOOD PREP
Making dinner and lunch for tomorrow takes time. If you're constantly staying at your significant other's place you probably aren't prepping food at home and instead buying food on the go. This not only puffs up your waistline but also drains your wallet.

I'm not a big fan of buying lunches. I've always eaten pretty healthy, so I really love making dinner at home and then taking my leftovers for lunch the next day. Just something easy like chicken, rice and vegetables. When I got into a relationship though and I was staying at his place, I couldn't very well take over my lunch for the next day to put in his fridge. I'm a bit of a weirdo, but I felt that was crossing a line. So, I would just buy lunch.

I'm much happier now, and I've saved quite a few pennies.

87.   NO FEEDBACK
Your other does something really annoying and you're being helpful by pointing it out. All of a sudden they get touchy and your conversation turns into an argument! It was just a little feedback, right? If you're flying solo you can avoid all that by being honest with yourself. After all, you have no bad qualities.

88.   MEMORY RETENTION
Your significant other probably has family, whose names you need to learn. If you forget a family member name it means you don't care about your other and you are a terrible listener and also a horrible person and may be sentenced to death. Okay so that may be slightly dramatic, but you get the point.

Personally, I have a huge family. It is hard enough for me to remember all of their names, let alone dive into learning a whole other family tree. At least when it's my own family they understand when I forget, since they know how complex and intricate our family tree is.

89.   BECOME A RANDOM ADVENTURER
It's Saturday and your friend wants you to go hiking on a 5 hour trek. Do you check in with your boyfriend? Fuck no, you don't need to. You throw on your runners, pack a granola bar, and hit the trail!

I would always talk about going on adventures with my ex. We wanted to do a big hike, or go on a weekend trip somewhere. For one reason or another it just didn't happen, and we didn't end up going. As soon as I was single though I didn't have to make plans, or arrange schedules. I just picked up and went. Out of all my friends there is usually at least one that is just ready to up and go!

90.   FAMILY VISITS AFAR
When you have family that lives far enough for you to need to hop on a flight to go see them, you want to see them often but you don't want to leave your significant other behind. You also don't have enough money to afford plane tickets for the both of you, so the number of visits is less than you would like.

When you're flying solo you can go for visits more often and spend time with the people in your life who matter most.

91.   KIDLETT RESPONSIBILITIES
So, sure, you could be single and still have little ones to take care of. This one is for those of us who are single and have not yet popped out the babies, or are old enough that they are grown and no longer need us to take care of them. There are a lot of great things about having kids, I am not saying they are bad. However, they sure are exhausting. If you're single and you have no kidletts, you don't need to worry about constant whining, or fighting, or 8am hockey practice

on Saturdays, or sugar intake, or... well, you get the point.

92.   SMOOTH RIDE

Chances are you and your significant other want to listen to different radio stations. I like country, he likes rock. There is a lot of compromise when it comes to music choices in the car, which can cause friction. Car rides are already annoying, especially if you are stuck in traffic or having to get somewhere quickly. You don't also want to have to listen to crappy music.

When I'm single I can blast whatever station I feel like listening to, or if I really want, I can just sit there in silence and listen to the road. That's kind of weird, but I have been known to do it just because I can.

93.   NO ANNOYING YOUR FRIENDS

Oh awesome, you and your boyfriend are fighting again. This time it is really over though, so you have to tell all of your friends how terrible he was and how you will never see him again. You whine for a while but eventually make up and get back together, so now your friends have to hear all about how he actually is a great person that deserves to be with you. After a few cycles of this your friends are either bored, annoyed, or no longer around.

Being single means you don't have the on-again-off-again relationship drama that your friends really don't want to hear about.

94.   FRIENDS GALORE
When you are in a relationship your friend circle dwindles. You spend most of your time with your significant other and all of a sudden you haven't seen your best friend Jane in over 6 months – where did the time go?

When you're single you have more time, which means more time to spend with friends and your circle just seems to naturally increase. Keep your friend circle luscious by living the single life.

95.   OWN YOUR OWN BELIEFS
I didn't realize how big an issue religion could be until I dated a Christian. I guess I have always dated atheists or agnostics because the issue of god never came up. I believe in a god, but I've never been to church and I am quite ignorant when it comes to religious beliefs – I suppose I have just never been in an environment to learn about them.

Dating a Christian wasn't too big a deal – he would go to church, I would stay home. When we went to his parents for dinner, I would sit with my head bowed while they prayed. I was interested in his beliefs, but not really sure if it was something I could adopt myself. After all, I didn't know anything about it. I began to feel anxiety about the whole situation. Does he want me to ask him about it? How do I act at church? Will our kids be brought up religious?

Being single, you don't have to stress over the religion of your significant other. You can own your own beliefs and hang out with friends who feel the same way. Anxiety free!

96. HOT WATER GALORE

You don't have to worry about jumping into the shower in the morning, only to find out that he put the laundry on, ran the dishes and then had an extra long morning shower to wake up, draining your hot water tank. An unpleasantly chilly morning wake-up indeed.

Sometimes I run the shower longer than I need to just because I can. Not the best idea in terms of water conservation, but it is definitely a guilty pleasure now that I am single.

97. NO ANNOYING FRIENDS

Your boyfriend probably had at least one friend that you were not fond of. The *bad influence*, who you associated with the word *strip club*, the *idiot*, who couldn't hold a conversation to save his life, or maybe the *gym bro*, who was always telling your man about new illicit substances that would help him get jacked. These friend types are annoying as hell and yet whenever you see them you have to act as though they are your favorite person or else you become the bitchy girlfriend.

When you're single you only have to be friends with the people you want.

98.   NOT THE MAMMA

With divorce rates on the rise and commitment levels at an all-time low, there are a significant number of split parents out there, which means that guy you're dating could very well have some kids of his own already. That means all of a sudden you aren't just a girlfriend, but a step-mom as well. That is fucking scary.

When you're single you avoid the mom drama until you're ready to pop out kids of your own.

99.   OBSESSION REMOVAL

My boyfriend seemed to take up a lot of my headspace. Whether it was thinking about what he would want for dinner, or being angry about something he had said, or planning out our work schedules to spend time together, I realized that I thought about him more than I even thought about myself and what I wanted. This took up a lot of time and brain resources, which could have been spent on more productive things.

Now that I am single I focus on myself, on my friends, on work, on adventures, on my health – you name it! The world is my oyster.

100.   ME TIME

I am very independent, and I like to spend my time alone. When I have a boyfriend I don't want to spend every moment with the other person, but I find that when I want distance they always think something is wrong.

I had a boyfriend who did shift work. He would work days and then nights, so on the night shifts I couldn't see him. This meant the time that we could spend together we had to spend together or else it would be a while until we saw each other again. Since we had to spend the time together it just didn't feel the same as spending time together because we wanted to.

Now that I'm single I have my alone time when I want it!

101. LIVE WHERE YOU WANT

If your significant other lives in a different city, all of a sudden a large part of your week is spent commuting. After a while *the talk* comes in about moving in together, and then you have to decide where to live.

I ended up moving into my boyfriend's place, which meant my commute to work went from 20 minutes to an hour each way, every weekday. It didn't really matter at first, but after a while that traffic started to really affect my mood. I felt as though my life was being wasted just sitting in traffic.

Now I live 5 minutes away from where I work, and I don't plan on moving any time soon.

About the author

Karleen Dee is a freelance writer from North Vancouver, British Columbia. She has been writing plays, poetry, and short stories since she was able to pick up a pen, writing and directing her first play at age eleven for her grade six class. Following seven years of University any many failed relationships, Karleen decided to put pen to paper, and with a humorous intellectual flair, she composed her first novel: 101 Reasons Why It's Great to Be Single.

CPSIA information can be obtained at www.ICGtesting.com
Printed in the USA
LVOW12s0609310115

425076LV00002B/46/P

9 781496 964311